If Only, If Only

Written and Illustrated by
Amanda Bower

This Book Belongs to:

_____

Once upon a time, there was a lovely little turtle named Jim. On one warm sunny afternoon, Jim was trotting around the riverbank when he noticed a blue jay flying overhead.

"I wish I could fly, fly high into the sky. If only, if only, I had magical wings to fly," Jim spoke as he watched the blue jay soaring above him. Suddenly, Jim had an idea. He foraged for some fallen leaves on the ground and taped them to his shell. He then climbed upon a boulder and flapped and flapped his arms into the air.

Unfortunately, Jim's makeshift wings failed him and he crashed against the grass. Jim was saddened to realize that he would never be able to fly, fly high into the sky.

Moments later, Jim happened upon a squirrel dashing up a tree.

"I wish I could climb, climb until the end of time. If only, if only, I had magical feet to climb," Jim spoke as he admired the squirrel hurrying up the tree trunk.

With much determination, Jim put all of his focus on his tiny turtle feet and attempted to climb up the tree.

Unfortunately, Jim's little legs grew tired of trying. Jim was utterly disappointed to realize that he would never be able to climb, climb until the end of time.

It was nearing lunchtime and Jim was meeting with his fox friend, Barb, for a picnic. Barb was fast and often sprinted round and round the river. Jim would usually cheer on his friend, but today Jim was sad because he was merely a slow-moving turtle.

"I wish I could dash, dash so fast that I'd be gone in a flash. If only, if only, I had magical legs to dash," Jim spoke as he admired Barb's speedy wit.

"Hey Barb," Jim said as Barb neared the riverbank, "do you want to race me?" Barb knew in her heart of hearts that Jim's little legs would not be able to keep up, but she loved her friend Jim and didn't want to let him down.

"Okay Jim!" Barb replied with a hint of nervousness in her voice.

As Jim began to run around the riverbank with Barb, he almost instantly realized that he would never be as swift and speedy as his friend. Jim felt discouraged.

"I wish I could fly, fly high into the sky. I wish I could climb, climb until the end of time. I wish I could dash, dash so fast that I'd be gone in flash. But I am simply a turtle, a turtle named Jim, and the only thing I can do is swim," Jim sadly spoke as he floated in the river.

"Boy, I sure wish I could swim, swim just like YOU, Jim. However, I cannot swim, for I am a fox, a fox that can only run. Don't you see? We are all extraordinary in our own ways, my friend," Barb spoke as she smiled down at Jim.

Quite suddenly, Jim was filled with joy. He was no longer sad that he could not fly, fly high into the sky. Or climb, climb until the end of time. Or dash, dash so fast that he'd be gone in a flash.

Jim no longer wanted to be a blue jay, a squirrel, or even a fox.

For the first time, Jim was happy being just as he was: a turtle.

CPSIA information can be obtained at www.ICGtesting.com
Printed in the USA
BVIW120028211019
561523BV00001BA/1